THE
TIE MAN'S
MIRACLE

A CHANUKAH TALE

by Steven Schnur
illustrated by Stephen T. Johnson

MORROW JUNIOR BOOKS
NEW YORK

GLOSSARY

Adonai (ah-doe-NIGH)—Hebrew term for God.

Chanukah (HA-nu-kah)—eight-day Jewish Festival of Lights celebrating the Maccabees' military victory and the rededication of the Holy Temple in Jerusalem. Gifts are often given during the holiday.

Maccabees (MAC-uh-bees)—warriors of the Hasmonean family of Israel who defeated occupying Syrian forces in 164 B.C.E. and ruled Israel for the next one hundred and thirty years.

menorah (meh-NAW-rah)—nine-branch candelabra lit at sundown on each of the eight nights of Chanukah. According to Jewish legend, a single cruse of consecrated oil, enough to last only one day, miraculously burned for eight days in the eternal light above the holy ark.

shammash (SHAH-maash)—the ninth candle that lights the other eight in the menorah. On the first night of Chanukah the shammash is used to light one candle, on the second night two, and on the last night all eight.

Watercolors were used for the full-color illustrations.
The text type is 17-point Weiss.

Printed in the United States of America.

1   2   3   4   5   6   7   8   9   10

Library of Congress Cataloging-in-Publication Data
Schnur, Steven.
The tie man's miracle: a Chanukah tale/by Steven Schnur; illustrated by Stephen T. Johnson.
p. cm.
Summary: On the last night of Chanukah, after hearing how an old man lost his family in the Holocaust, a young boy makes a wish that is carried to God as the menorah candles burn down.
ISBN 0-688-13463-7 (trade)—ISBN 0-688-13464-5 (library)
[1. Hanukkah—Fiction.   2. Jews—Fiction.]   I. Johnson, Stephen, ill.   II. Title.   PZ7.S3644Ti 1995   [E]—dc20   94-39854   CIP AC

For Dad
May the miracles never cease
—S.S.

To Debbie and her wonderful family
—S.T.J.

It had just begun to snow when a bent little man limped up our front path, carrying a tattered cardboard box wound around and around with twine. I was standing by the window waiting for Dad to get home so we could light the Chanukah candles.

"Mr. Hoffman's coming," I called to Mom.

She joined me at the window and sighed, then hurried upstairs for her purse, telling me to let him in. When I opened the door Mr. Hoffman bowed and asked in a thick accent, "Is your mother home, please?" His eyes were so dark they seemed almost hollow.

"She'll be right down," I answered. Despite the cold he wasn't wearing an overcoat or boots, just a rumpled gray suit and hat. "Aren't you freezing?" I asked, closing the door behind him.

"I've been much colder," he replied, laying his cardboard box on the kitchen table. He blew on his fingers a moment, then

began untying the knotted twine. "How old are you now, fine
boy?" he asked.

"Seven," I answered.

"Seven?" he replied, studying me a moment. "So tall! Your
parents must be very proud."

Mom entered the room holding Hannah in her arms. Mr. Hoffman bowed again, then fixed his eyes on my baby sister and declared, "Such a jewel!" Hannah gurgled at him.

"Are you working so late on Chanukah?" Mom asked, glancing at the clock.

"A man has to eat," he replied softly, "even during the holidays. Just a minute of your time, please."

"Isn't your family waiting for you?" I asked, afraid he was going to delay our celebration.

He stared at me a moment, then shook his head and said, "I have no family."

Before I could ask why not, he removed the top of his cardboard box, revealing hundreds of colorful ties. One by one he held them up, knotting them around his fingers, draping them over his arm, laying them across the table. "This with a blue suit would be very nice," he suggested. "Or perhaps a paisley." Though he promised to stay only a minute, he spent almost half an hour with Mom.

When Dad finally came up the walk, I ran out to meet him, asking impatiently, "Can we light the candles now?"

"As soon as I take my coat off." He kissed the top of my head.

Mr. Hoffman was just beginning to knot up his box as we joined him. "Would you have a look?" he asked, hurrying to untie the twine.

"Thank you," Dad replied, picking up the five ties Mom had bought, "but I don't think I can improve on these. Why don't you join us while we light the menorah?"

"I've already taken too much of your time," Mr. Hoffman said, retying the box.

"It'll only take a minute," Dad insisted, "and then I'll drive you wherever you need to go. It's snowing pretty hard out."

"Thank you, but I can't."

I took Dad's hand and tried to pull him toward the living room
and the waiting menorah. But then my little sister began to cry.

"What's the matter, Hannah?" Mom cooed.

Mr. Hoffman looked up from the tie box, his dark eyes
gleaming. "Hannalah?" he whispered. He moved a little closer,

repeating her name softly. It seemed to calm her.

"Come, we'll light the candles together," Dad said, laying his hand on the tie man's forearm.

"Well, maybe for just a minute," Mr. Hoffman murmured, his eyes filled with Hannah.

When we were all standing before the menorah, Dad lit the shammash, the candle that lights all the others, and handed it to our guest, asking, "Would you do us the honor?"

But Mr. Hoffman shook his head and backed away. "I can't," he whispered. "Let the children."

Dad looked at Mom, then passed the shammash to me. While the tie man stood silently in the shadows, I lit the eight remaining candles and chanted the Hebrew prayer: "Blessed are You, Adonai our God, ruler of the universe, who long ago performed miracles for our ancestors at this season."

"Amen," Mr. Hoffman whispered.

"Happy Chanukah!" Dad announced, handing me a large box. For the next several minutes I forgot about our guest. And then I heard Mom ask, "Are you all right?" I looked up to see Mr. Hoffman watching Hannah, his eyes brimming with tears.

"Excuse me. I must go, it's late," he said.

"Let me drive you," Dad insisted.

"No, I couldn't, thank you," he replied, stepping away from us. I wanted to take his hand and pull him back. But before I could he turned and limped to the kitchen for his box.

"Why is he so sad?" I asked.

Mom shushed me, looking toward the kitchen.

"How come he doesn't have any family?" I pursued.

Mr. Hoffman appeared in the doorway, his cardboard box under his arm. "I had a family once," he answered quietly, "a very big family."

"What happened to them?" I asked.

"Seth, please," Mom interrupted, her cheeks reddening.

"A sad story," the tie man said. "This is supposed to be a happy night."

"It's also a night for remembering," Dad said, offering him a chair. "Please."

Mr. Hoffman hesitated, then sat at the very edge of the cushion, resting the box on his knees. Mom and I settled onto the couch with Hannah between us.

"Long ago, before you were born," he began sadly, "I had a boy your age. Shmuel, Samuel as you say here, was my oldest, seven years, just like you. But he was not so tall. His younger brother, Isaac, was to be the tall one." He paused a moment, lost in thought.

"Any girls?" Mom asked.

"Three," he replied slowly. "Sarah, Leah, and my own little Hannalah." He reached inside his jacket and removed a torn and faded photograph of himself sitting stiffly beside a young woman holding a newborn baby. Two small girls dressed in white sat at his feet. Two older boys stood behind him.

"Why aren't you celebrating Chanukah with them?" I asked. "Do they live far away?"

The tie man nodded his head slowly. "Yes, very far."

"Where?" I asked.

"They're gone," he replied gravely. "I lost them in the war."

Mom put her hand to her mouth.

"How?" I asked. How could someone lose his whole family and not find them again?

"How?" he replied sadly. "Only God can answer that question."

"We've never spoken to Seth of that time," Dad said gently, looking at me.

"Forgive me," the tie man apologized.

Dad took my hand. "Before you were born," he began to explain, "there was a terrible war. Many people were killed, especially Jewish people."

"Even children?" I asked, thinking about Mr. Hoffman's family.

"Even children," he replied.

Outside the wind hurled clouds of snow against the window. Mr. Hoffman rose. "I must go."

"I'm sorry," Dad said. "We didn't mean to cause you pain."

"You caused nothing," the tie man replied softly. "They are never out of my thoughts."

"Of course they aren't," Mom said sadly.

Mr. Hoffman bowed and turned toward the door.

"Won't you eat something with us first?" Mom pleaded. "A little soup? It's so cold out."

He looked toward the window, then at Hannah and me. "A little soup would be nice. Thank you."

While Mom filled our bowls the tie man watched Hannah crawl across the floor. When we all were served, he bowed his head a moment and muttered a brief prayer, then picked up his spoon and began to eat. He ate slowly, as though he could feel every spoonful warming and strengthening him. After finishing he leaned toward me and said, "Before I go, let me tell you a happy tale.

"In our village," he began, "we believed that every Chanukah was a time of miracles, just as it had been for the Maccabees. On the eighth night we didn't just light the menorah but watched the candles burn all the way down, believing that if they all went out at exactly the same instant, those nine little columns of smoke would rise as one up to heaven, carrying our wishes straight to the ear of God." He held out his hands, palms up, and slowly raised his fingers toward the ceiling. "It had to be all nine candles. Nothing less could travel so far."

"Did they ever all go out together?" I asked.

He shook his head. "I never saw it. Usually the shammash died first, then one by one the other eight." He leaned closer and whispered, "But you never know. Watch them carefully. Perhaps tonight your dreams will come true."

"Why don't you stay and see for yourself?" Dad suggested.

"Thank you," he replied, rising, "but now I must go."

"Please stay," I pleaded. "Don't you have a wish?"
"I'm afraid my wish is too heavy even for all nine candles."
He looked at Hannah one last time. "Take care of your little

sister." Then he leaned down and stroked her cheek. Hannah cooed at him, and for just a moment the tie man smiled, his eyes glistening as brightly as the candles.

Later, while Mom and Dad put Hannah to bed, I returned to the darkened living room. The nine candles had burned down to the menorah itself, each one nothing more than a tiny black wick surrounded by a small blue flame. I wanted to shout to Mom and Dad to come look but was afraid if I stirred one of them would go out before the others, breaking the spell.

In the fading light I silently wished, Please give the tie man back his family.

The shammash flickered, then so did the other eight candles. I held my breath. A moment later the room went black. Nine narrow columns of smoke rose from the silver menorah. A little way above my head they seemed to join in a delicate braid, rising faster. Suddenly the room grew bright. I heard voices shouting, "Papa, Papa!" Shadows danced on the ceiling, feet scurried across the floor, laughter filled the air. And then all was silent and dark.

Spring came and then summer and finally the cold, but not the tie man. Every time the doorbell rang I ran to answer it, hoping to find him standing there with his cardboard box. But he never returned, and not since that snowy evening have I seen all nine candles burn out together. Still, every year Hannah and I look forward to the eighth night with special excitement. Sitting before the menorah, our heads resting in our hands, we whisper our secret dreams as the tiny blue flames burn down and disappear in a flicker of light and a whirl of smoke.

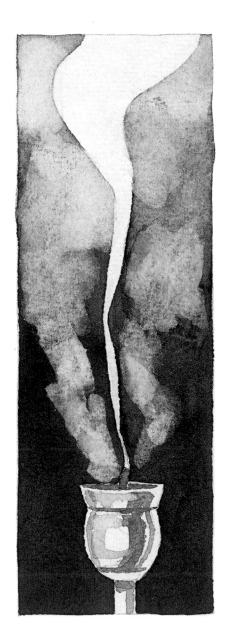